For Zachary and Mylo Layden-Thompson

First published in 2019 in Great Britain by
Barrington Stoke, 18 Walker Street, Edinburgh, EH3 7LP

www.barringtonstoke.co.uk

Text & Illustrations © 2019 Kate Milner

The moral right of Kate Milner to be identified as the
author and illustrator of this work has been asserted
in accordance with the Copyright, Designs and Patents
Act, 1988

A CIP catalogue record for this book is available
from the British Library upon request

ISBN: 978-1-78112-881-7

Printed in Turkey by Imago

Kate Milner

It's a No-Money Day

Barrington Stoke

Wake up, Mum. I'm hungry!

There's no more cereal,
so I have the last piece of toast.

Luckily Mum isn't hungry.

Mum works hard so we can buy the things we need.

I look after the everything-else jar.

Mum says that if it ever gets full, we can get a kitten.

Maybe one day.

But today is a no-money day.

There are still fun things you can do on a no-money day.

You can read a book
from the library. The scary
ones are the best.

You can practise your singing
in case you get on the telly.

You can make a cat out of
your mum's dressing gown.

You can call it Janet
if you want.

You can chase the pigeons.

You can try things on in the charity shop.

Luckily Mum and me are very good at fashion.

But today we have to go to the foodbank.

Mum doesn't like going to the foodbank but I do.

I can have biscuits and squash and tell the lady
all about the kitten we might get.

Mum gets cross when I ask the lady if I can have my favourite cereal.

The lady says she's sorry but she can only give me what kind people give to the foodbank.

On the way home me and Mum
play the maybe-one-day game.

"Maybe one day," Mum says.

I say, "Maybe one day."

Maybe one day me and Mum won't have to worry, but tonight, because of kind people, our tummies are full.

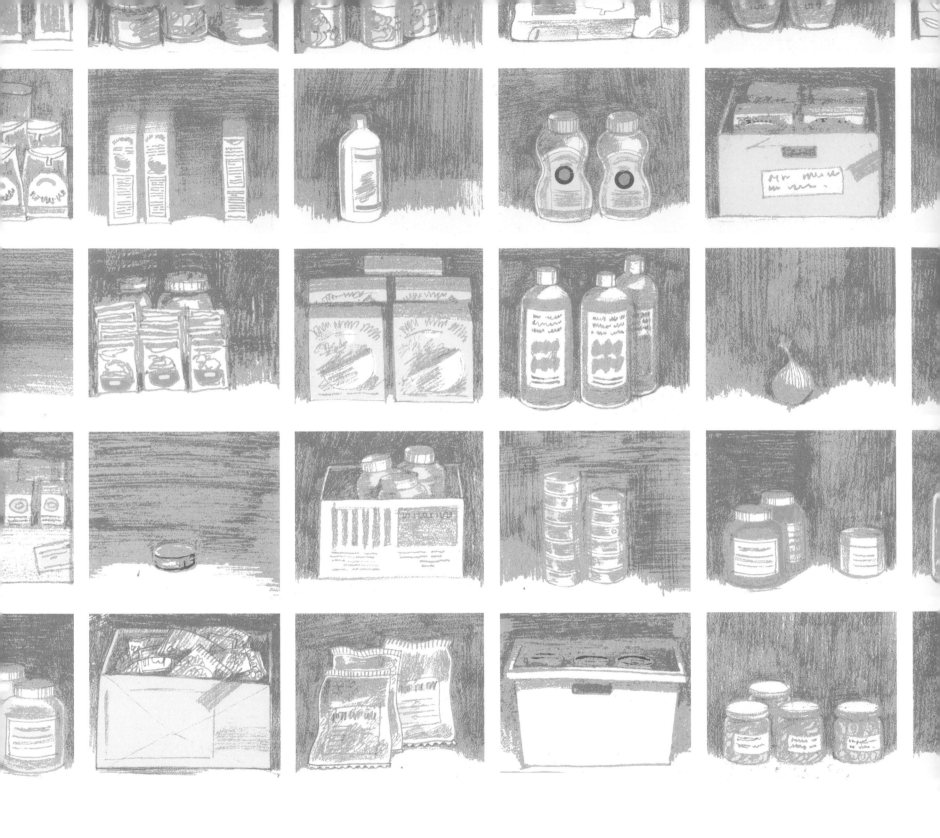

It's a No-Money Day

For the Auntorage

First published 2018 by Walker Books Ltd, 87 Vauxhall Walk, London SE11 5HJ

This edition published 2019

2 4 6 8 10 9 7 5 3 1

© 2018 Daisy Hirst

This book has been typeset in WB Natalie Alphonse

Printed in China

British Library Cataloguing in Publication Data: a catalogue record for this book is available from the British Library

ISBN 978-1-4063-8291-4

www.walker.co.uk

I DO NOT LIKE BOOKS ANYMORE!

Daisy Hirst

WALKER BOOKS
AND SUBSIDIARIES
LONDON · BOSTON · SYDNEY · AUCKLAND

NATALIE and ALPHONSE
really liked books
and stories.

Picture books with Dad,

scary books Mum read when Alphonse was sleeping,

Granny's stories about Melvin Plant Pot and the Terrible Shrew,

and stories
they remembered

or made up.

Natalie said,
"When I can read,
I'll have all the stories in
the world, whenever I want them."

"And you can read them to me!" said Alphonse.

Then Natalie got her first reading book.

"There's a cat in it!" said Natalie. "I will read it all by myself."

But when she opened the book ...

the letters and words looked
like prickles or birds' feet.

Miss Bimble said, "It just takes practice." She helped Natalie to sound out the words. The book was about a cat. The cat could sit.

Natalie tried
to read the
book to Mum.

"I can't," said Natalie. "And nothing
even happens to the cat! I like
you and Dad to read to me."

"You will be able to," said Mum.

Dad said, "And the books
will get better."

Natalie practised her reading book all week. Again and again and again, until she knew all the words.

"Do you know how
to read about trains
please and bears?"
said Alphonse.

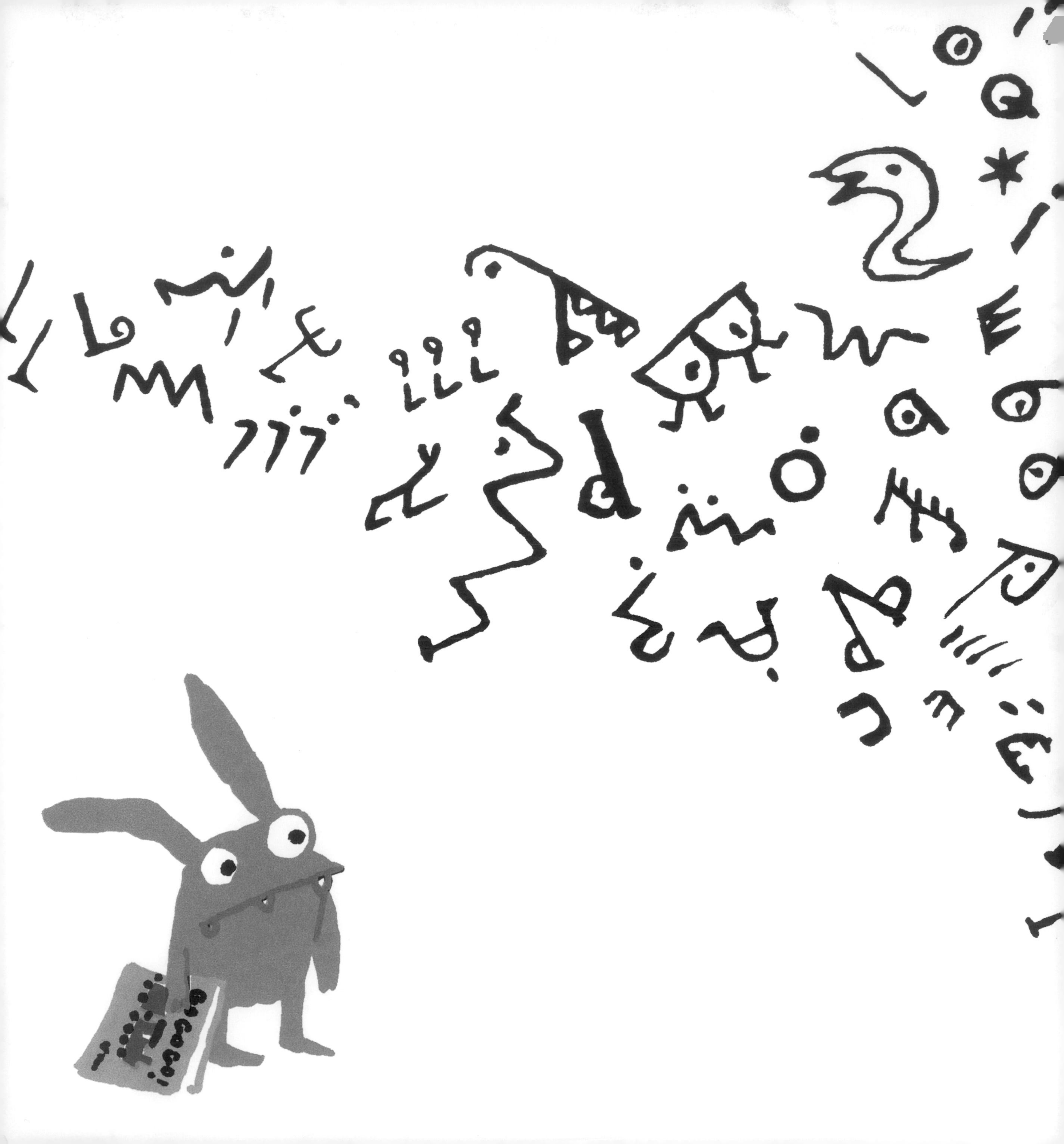

But the letters and words in Alphonse's book looked like scuttling insects, with too many legs and eyes.

Natalie said, **"NO."**

"I DO NOT
LIKE BOOKS
ANYMORE!"

"I can't learn to read anymore," said Natalie. "Sinéad is sick and I have to look after her."

"Poor Sinéad," said Mum. "But you can still read."

"I don't need to," said Natalie. "I can make my own stories and tell them to Alphonse."

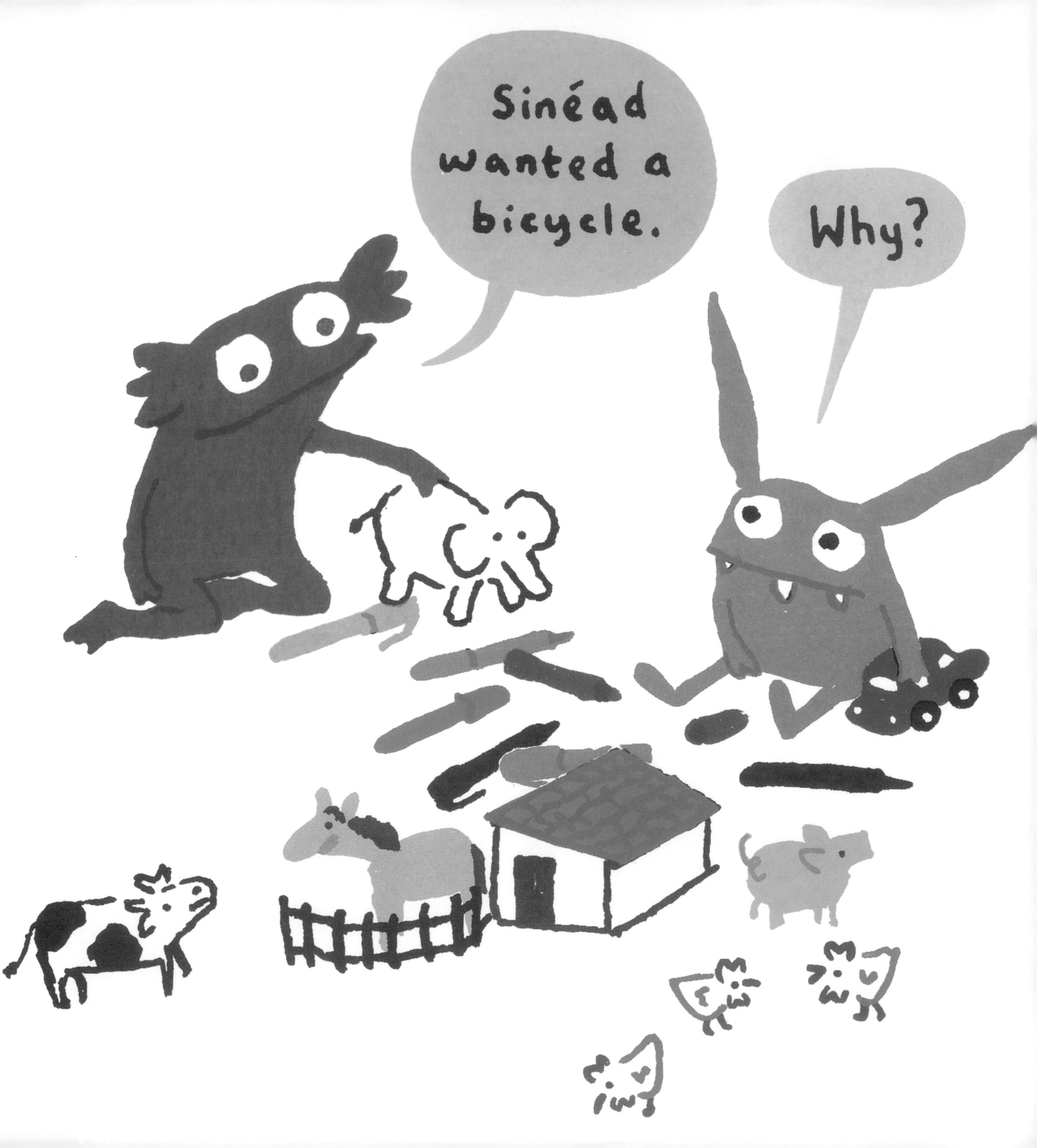
Sinéad wanted a bicycle.
Why?

To go to the farm to see chickens. But she didn't have any money so she had to get a job.

What job?

Cleaning up pens.

Then a caterpillar came in a truck!

Ok. A caterpillar came in a truck and ran over the pens.

And it was a MESS and a DISASTER.

Sinéad was so angry, she said, "Eric! You ruined my job! Now how can I buy a bicycle and go to the farm?"

Is Eric the caterpillar's name?

Yes. Eric said, "I know! You can ride in my truck to see the chickens!" And they drove away. Honking the horn.

"It's a good story," said Alphonse.
"It should be in a book."

"Why?" said Natalie.

"So we could have it again.
And with pictures."

"Let's draw the pictures
anyway," Natalie said.

Then Natalie told Dad what the words should say, and they stapled it into a book.

"Now can you tell it to me again?" said Alphonse.

A Caterpillar Came
in a Truck

And Natalie
found that,
mostly,
she could
read the
book they'd
written

(with Alphonse helping).

ALSO BY DAISY HIRST:

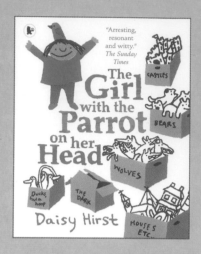

978-1-4063-6552-8

"Arresting, resonant and witty" *The Sunday Times*, Children's Book of the Week

Shortlisted for the Klaus Flugge Prize and the Sheffield Children's Book Award

978-1-4063-7831-3

"A sweet story of an unexpected friendship" *BookTrust*

"An unusual gem of a book, full of charm and humour" *LoveReading4Kids*

Available from all good booksellers www.walker.co.uk

This Walker

book belongs to:

_____

_____

_____